MRS. McCool AND THE GIANT CUHULLIN

An Irish Tale

Jessica Souhami

Henry Holt and Company • New York

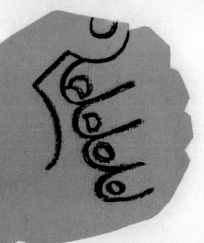

Long ago there lived a giant called Cuhullin. My, but he was big and fierce and strong. And what made him so strong? He had a magic finger. And believe it or not, all his strength was in that little finger.

Now, Cuhullin had fought all the other giants, and squashed them flat. Well, all but one, and that was Finn McCool.

"Where is that Finn McCool?" he said. "When I find him—

POW! WHAM!—flat as a pancake he'll be. That'll prove I'm the strongest giant in the world."

And off he went in search of Finn.

What was he like, this Finn McCool? And where was he all this while? Was he spoiling for a fight?

Well, that huge Finn was lying low and sucking his thumb!

But then, Finn's thumb was magic. When he sucked it Finn could see what would happen next. And he could see Cuhullin coming to get him.

"Oh dear!" he cried. "Not that I'm scared of that old Cuhullin. Not at all! Well . . . perhaps just the tiniest, littlest bit scared. What shall I do?" And poor Finn trembled. "I'd best go home to my dear wife, Oona. She's got me out of trouble many times before."

So Finn set out for his house on the hill where Oona was waiting to welcome him.

Finn told Oona all about Cuhullin.

"Keep calm, Finn," she said. "I'll think of something. Just suck your magic thumb to see when Cuhullin will arrive."

Finn sucked his thumb. **"Today, Oona!"** he called out. **"Today!"**

"Hmm," said Oona. "And when today?"

Finn sucked his thumb again. **"This afternoon!"**

"Hmm," said Oona. "And what time this afternoon?"

Finn sucked harder. **"At four o'clock!"**

"Four o'clock?" said Oona. **"That's TEA-TIME!"**

She started to laugh. "I've such a plan, Finn!" she said.

And Oona set to work.

Oona started by making some bread. She made enough dough for two big round loaves. She left one plain, but in the other she placed an **iron griddle**—the iron griddle that she usually heated on the fire to cook pancakes. And when the two loaves came out of the oven they looked exactly the same.

Then Oona hid Finn in a giant baby's cradle. Well, all of him that would fit inside. And she put a baby's bonnet on his head. Then they waited for Cuhullin.

They waited . . . and they waited. . . .

And just as the clock was striking four, there was a great banging at the door.

"Do come in!" said brave Oona McCool.

And in came the giant Cuhullin.

"Is Finn McCool at home?" he boomed.

"No," said Oona calmly. "There's just me . . . and the baby. Finn's out looking for some big silly called Cuhullin who wants to fight him. Poor Cuhullin! Finn'll make mincemeat of him!"

And she smiled up at Cuhullin.

"BUT I'M CUHULLIN!"

"Bah!" said Oona scornfully, looking him up and down. "You've not met my Finn! Well, you can wait for him if you dare, and I'll brew some tea. But first, will you do a small job for me? Will you lift the house so I can sweep the dust from under it? Finn does it every day."

What a storyteller that Oona was!

Cuhullin was astonished.

"Well, if Finn can do it, so can I!" he said.

And he went outside.

Cuhullin stretched out his brawny arms and gripped the house.

He **heaved** and **shoved**,
and **grunted** and **groaned**,
and **grunted** and **shoved**,
and **heaved** and **groaned**.

And just as he felt he must burst, the house began to move.

And Oona calmly swept the dust from under it as if the house was lifted up every day.

"This Finn must be mighty strong," muttered Cuhullin.

Meanwhile Finn, hiding in the cradle, trembled and shook from head to foot.

"Thank you, dear man," said Oona. "Now if you'll just fill the kettle from the spring, I'll make the tea."

Cuhullin looked out. "Where is the spring, Mrs. McCool?" he asked.

"It's under that pebble," replied Oona, pointing to a huge boulder. "Finn lifts it to get water every day."

What a storyteller that Oona was!

Cuhullin was astonished.

"That pebble's a mountain!" he said. "But if Finn can do it, so can I!" He went down the hill and put his huge shoulders to the boulder.

Cuhullin **heaved** and **shoved**, and **grunted** and **groaned**, and **grunted** and **shoved**, and **heaved** and **groaned**.

And just as he felt he must burst, the boulder began to move.

Oona was as calm as if the boulder was lifted every day. But Cuhullin, wearily filling the kettle, was thinking, "Could this Finn be stronger than I am?"

Meanwhile Finn, hiding in the cradle, trembled and shook from head to foot.

At last Cuhullin sat down for tea. . . .

"Do have one of my home-baked loaves," said Oona. And she gave Cuhullin the loaf with the griddle inside. He took a big bite.

"**Aaaaargh!**" he yelled. "I can't eat this, Mrs. McCool. It'll break all my teeth. It's as hard as iron!"

"But it's Finn's favorite bread, Mr. Cuhullin," said Oona. "Finn and even the baby eat it every day."

What a storyteller that Oona was!

Just then Finn called out, as if he really was a baby, *"Wah! Wah! Mama! Hungry, Mama!"*

"Oh see now, Mr. Cuhullin," said Oona trying not to laugh. "You've woken the baby. Just give him that other loaf, if you please."

And Cuhullin did as she asked. But remember, this was a proper loaf. There was no griddle inside.

Finn ate the loaf in three bites!

"Yum-yum, Mama!" he said. "All gone!"

Cuhullin was astonished. If the baby could eat this bread, what could Finn do?

And should he stay to find out?

Just then Finn sat up.

"GOODNESS!" exclaimed Cuhullin. "Look at the size of him! Look at that mustache! If this is the baby, what must Finn be like?"

He moved to the door. "I really must be going, Mrs. McCool," he mumbled.

"Oh dear," said Oona calmly. "Finn will be sorry to have missed you. Before you go, just see what lovely teeth my baby's growing. Feel his little gums."

"Just to please you, Mrs. McCool," said Cuhullin. "And then I'll be off."

Cuhullin leaned over the cradle and put his little finger—
his magic little finger—into Finn's mouth.

And guess what?

SNAP!
Finn bit it off!

And with a whoosh,
Cuhullin started to shrink.
He got tinier
and tinier,
and teenier
and teenier,
and he ran right out of the house . . .
. . . and he hopped and he jumped and he skipped down
the hill and he ran far away and was never, ever seen again.
And as for Finn and Oona . . .

. . . they laughed and they laughed.

"Oona, my clever wife," said Finn. "You've saved me once again."

"It was nothing, dear Finn," said Oona. "Big is big. But brains are better!"

They danced and they danced . . . and if I'm not wrong, they are laughing and dancing still.

About the Story

This Irish tale makes fun of two of the greatest heroes of Celtic legend—Cuhullin and Finn McCool—who could never have met. Cuhullin's tales are told in the Ulster Cycle of the first century A.D., while Finn McCool's legends appear in the Fenian Cycle of the third century A.D. This tale possibly dates from the sixteenth century when comic parodies of the heroic legends started to appear. In the nineteenth century, when the study of Irish folklore began to flourish, several versions were collected, including William Carleton's 1846 version on which Joseph Jacobs based his 1892 retelling. This version is a very loose adaptation of the tale.

Henry Holt and Company, LLC, *Publishers since 1866*
115 West 18th Street, New York, New York 10011

Henry Holt is a registered trademark of Henry Holt and Company, LLC
Copyright © 2002 Frances Lincoln Limited
Text, illustrations, and design copyright © 2002 by Jessica Souhami and Paul McAlinden
All rights reserved.
First published in the United States in 2002 by Henry Holt and Company, LLC
Distributed in Canada by H. B. Fenn and Company Ltd.
Originally published in Great Britain in 2002 by Frances Lincoln Limited

Library of Congress Cataloging-in-Publication Data
Souhami, Jessica. Mrs. McCool and the giant Cuhullin: an Irish tale / Jessica Souhami.
Summary: The very clever Oona saves her husband, the giant Finn McCool, by outwitting
Cuhullin, who seeks to prove that he is the strongest giant in the world by beating Finn.
1. Finn MacCumhaill, 3rd cent.–Legends. [1. Finn MacCool–Legends. 2. Folklore–Ireland.]
I. Title. PZ8.1.S706 Mr 2002 398.2'09417'01–dc21 2001002884

ISBN 0-8050-6852-X / First American Edition–2002 / Design by Donna Mark
Printed in Singapore
10 9 8 7 6 5 4 3 2 1